THE MOLE SI...
and the Fairy Ring

Roslyn Schwartz

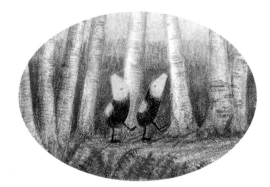

ZERO TO TEN

First published in Great Britain in 2005
by Zero To Ten,
part of Evans Publishing Group
2A Portman Mansions
Chiltern Street
London W1U 6NR

Originally published in North America by Annick Press Ltd.
© 2003 Roslyn Schwartz/Annick Press Ltd.
This edition © 2005 Zero To Ten Ltd

British Library Cataloguing in Publication Data
Schwartz, Roslyn
The mole sisters and the fairy ring
1. Mole sisters (Fictitious characters) - Pictorial works - Juvenile fiction
2. Children's stories - Pictorial works
I. Title
813.5'4 [J]

ISBN 1 84089 384 2

Printed in China

To Gabrielle Bliss

"Look!" said the mole sisters.

"Over there."

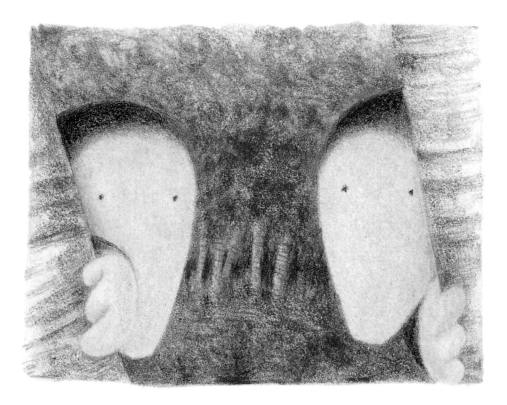

"See?"

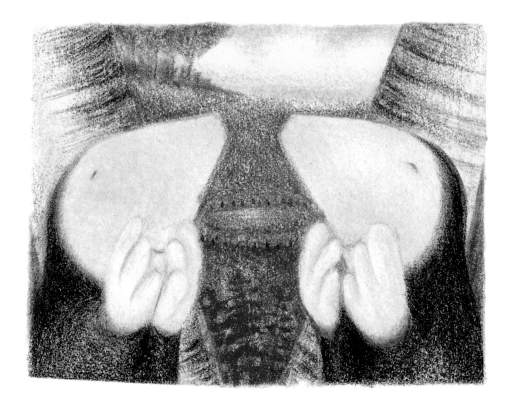

"It's a... it's a..."

"Fairy ring!"

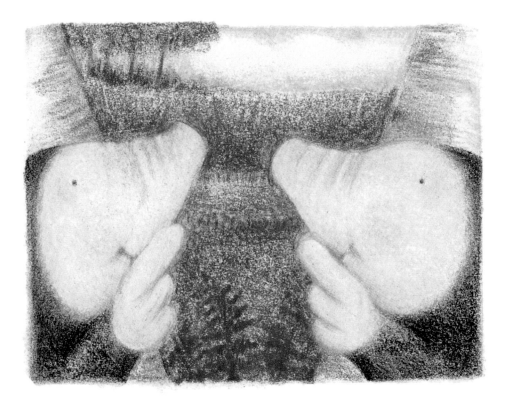

"Sssssh."

"The fairies don't know we're here."

"Let's sneak up on them."

"Hee hee, sneak sneak."

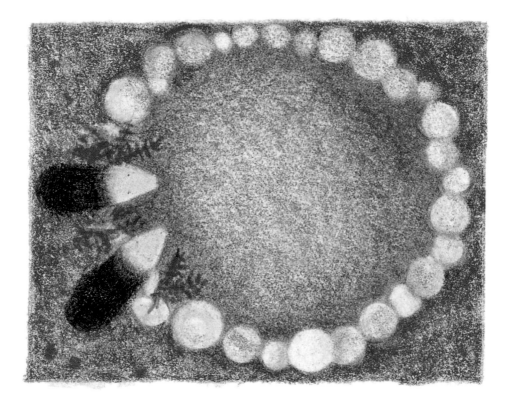

"Oh!"

"No one home."

"Never mind," said the mole sisters.

"Let's be fairies!"

"Okey-dokey."

"How do we look?"

"All we need is fairy dust..."

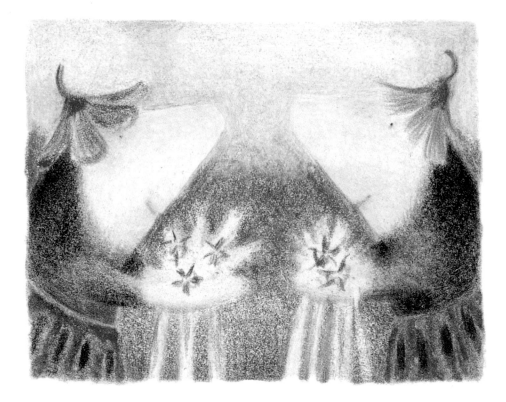

Twinkle twinkle

"...and voilà!"

"we look just like fairies!"

Flit flit

whizz

Bang.

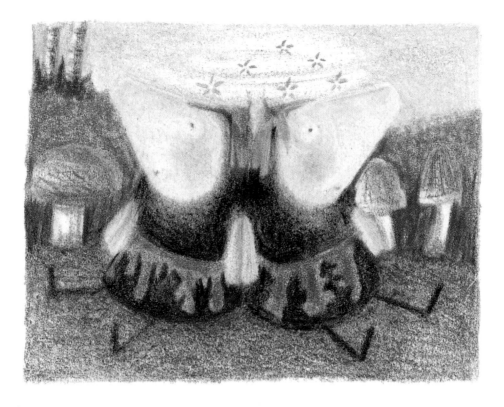

whoomph!

"Whew."

"Enough of that,"
said the mole sisters.

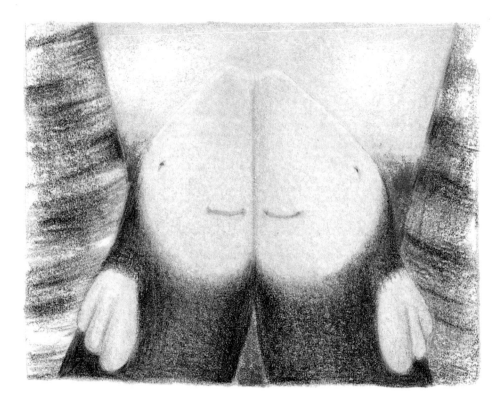

"Let's be moles."

And they were!

More books about the Mole Sisters:

The Mole Sisters and the Rainy Day
The Mole Sisters and the Wavy Wheat
The Mole Sisters and the Moonlit Night